The Magical Tale of Santa Dust®

A Christmas Tradition

Written by: Patricia Cardello
Illustrated by: Manuela Soriani

This book belongs to: ———————————————

I began my Santa Dust tradition on: ———————————

N & J Publishing
New York

Once upon a Christmas Eve, on a quiet street where street lamps seldom flickered, a boy and his sister sat looking out their window at the darkening sky that Santa would be flying across later that night on his magical flight.

"It's time for all good little boys and girls to be in bed now," came a soft, quiet voice from outside their door.

The children left their spot at the window and climbed into bed.

"Do you think this will be the year Santa visits us, Mother?" blurted the boy, startling his sister and waking Jack, a scruffy little white dog who slept curled up by their door.

"We hardly have enough wood to keep warm," answered his sister. "We could never build a fire bright enough for Santa to be able to see our house."

The boy looked at his mother and she nodded. "I'm sorry sweetheart—maybe next year."

Tears stung the boy's eyes and he fought to keep them from spilling onto his cheeks.

"But we've been so good," he said.

"You are always good," his mother replied. "If Santa knew you were here, I'm sure he would bring you all the presents you deserve."

The boy turned to face the wall so his mother and sister wouldn't see him cry. His mother bent to kiss him on the cheek.

"Good night, Children," said their mother.

That night, as the boy slept, dreaming of elves and presents, a strange
noise awakened him.

He opened his eyes to find Jack, pawing at the window, whimpering at
something outside.

The boy looked out the window into the faint moonlight, but saw only
the silhouettes of trees and the hard-packed snow on the ground.

"Hush, Jack," the boy scolded, but the dog wouldn't be quiet.

So the boy pulled his thin coat over his pajamas to carry Jack outside.

No sooner had the boy opened the door, when Jack leapt from his arms and ran full speed into the bushes.

"Jack, Jack!" the boy called in a loud whisper. But the boy heard nothing but silence.

Suddenly Jack came bursting out of the bushes and jumped into his young master's arms.

Jack was wet from the snow and the boy began to shiver. But as he held his breath in the quiet of the night, he heard a happy little voice giggling in the bushes Jack had just come out of—followed by the sound of tiny little feet running across the snow.

The boy turned and fled into the house.

"Where have you been?" asked
his sister as he burst into the room.

"Jack heard something outside..." began
the boy when he was interrupted by his sister.

"What's in Jack's mouth?" she cried excitedly.

In the dog's mouth was a fancy red pouch tied with a red braided cord.
It looked expensive and out of place in their modest room.

"Let's open it," said the boy.

"I'm not going to touch it," his sister protested, "it has Jack's drool on it."

The boy abruptly snatched it from the dog's mouth.

Slowly, the boy pulled back the cord. As the pouch fell open, a bright light flashed before his eyes.

He reached inside the pouch and pulled out a silver glass ball covered in snowflake designs that seemed to move as they sparkled, lighting up the room.

"What is it?" whispered his sister.

"I don't know," said the boy. "It looks like a Christmas tree ornament, full of some kind of dust."

"It's so beautiful," said the girl. "But how does it sparkle so bright with so little light?"

"It must be magical!" said the boy.

Then the girl got an idea. "If we can hang it from the highest peek on the chimney outside–Santa will see the sparkle and is sure to find us!" the girl exclaimed excitedly.

She grabbed her brothers coat and handed it to him.

"Santa is going to come, brother. I believe Santa will find us," said the girl in awe as she and Jack climbed into the boys red sled.

The boy didn't reply–not wanting to get his hopes up.

"This is a good spot to climb onto the roof,"
said the boy, rubbing his hands together.

"Give me the ornament."

But when his sister was taking the ornament out of its pouch, it slipped from her fingers and burst onto the ground with a surprising little *pop*.

The boy and girl stared down as a shimmering silver dust, all that was left of the ornament, floated around the ground, where it stayed, sparkling in the moonlight.

"Oh no!" cried the girl. "Now Santa will never find us."

Later that night, as the two children and their dog lay sleeping in their beds, Santa's sleigh flew swiftly thru the night sky on his yearly journey overhead.

"Whoa, Rudolph!" Santa cried out when he spotted a familiar sparkling in the darkness below.

And he shook his reins—guiding his reindeer down for a closer look.

That was when Santa saw a
house he had never seen before.

He brought his sleigh to a full stop on the snow-packed roof and, on silent footsteps, he shimmied down the chimney, his magical sack over his shoulder.

Inside the house Santa found the red velvet pouch where the boy had left it.

"Oh, my!" said Santa, "one of my elves must have lost their magical ornament!"

Santa opened his sack, reached in, and pulled out a fat little Christmas tree, complete with decorations, and placed it in a dusty corner of the room.

He then took out five presents, one for each member of the family—including a bone for Jack.

Then, almost as an afterthought, Santa took a small card out of his pocket. When he blew on it—dust sprinkled down.

As Santa reached out to collect the dust, a poem appeared in tiny gold letters:

Sprinkle on the ground at night
The moon will make it sparkle bright
Santa's reindeer fly and roam
this will lead him to your home!

Santa collected the dust and poured it into the red pouch.
He then attached the card to the pouch and hung it onto the tree.

"Santa Dust!" he said, tapping the pouch with his finger.

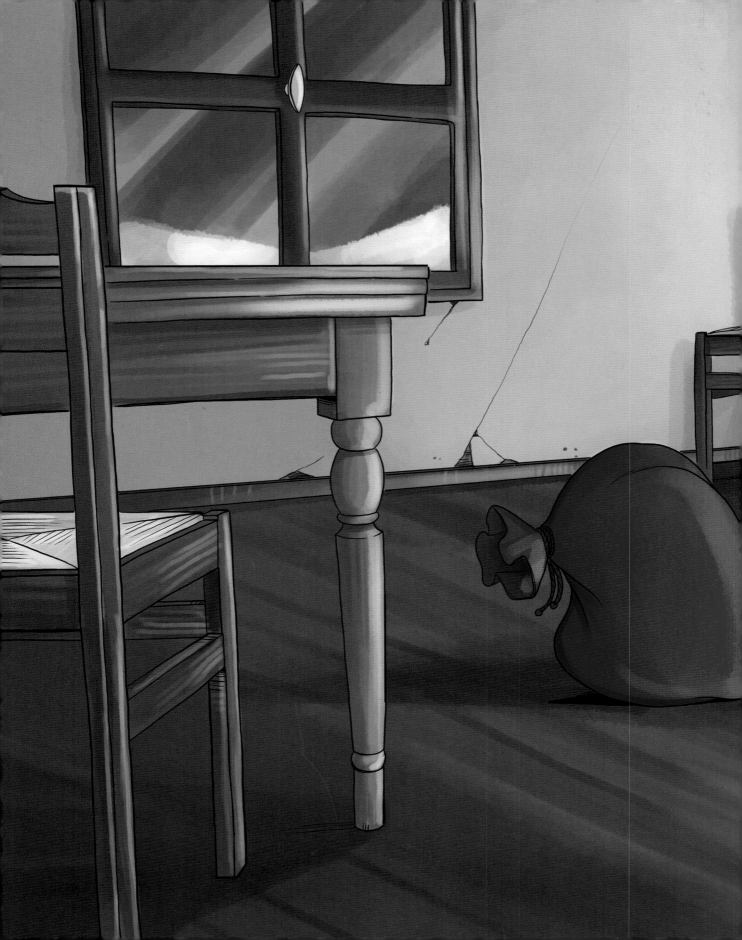

Then, just as Santa was turning to leave,
Jack ran into the room to investigate.

Santa put his finger to his lips and Jack
seemed to understand that—all was well.

After Santa left, Jack ran back into the children's bedroom and hopped into the little boy's bed.

That night Jack slept soundly knowing that, in the morning, the children would be waking to their very first visit from Santa.

And, as Jack fell asleep, he wondered how many other little boys and girls around the world, would be waking on Christmas morning to

The Magic of Santa Dust

Believe

To Bob, Nicole & Jenna
In memory of Mom & Dad - with love forever.

First Edition
Library of Congress Control Number: 2011904212 - ISBN: 978-0-9833662-0-1

Illustrations and Interior Design: Manuela Soriani - arcemproject@yahoo.it

"Santa Dust" and "The Magical Tale of Santa Dust - A Christmas Tradition" are registered trademarks of PAC Jennic Inc.

Printed in The United States of America

N & J Publishing
197 Prince Street, Suite #2 New York, New York 10012, 212-260-7075, 212-330-7708
NandJPublishing@aol.com themagicaltale@aol.com www.magicdusts.com